Anahita,

Always remember these beautiful pictures that hung in your school oops

Happy 7th Birthday.

Love you,

Gramma and Papa

Seasons of Joy

Every Day is for Outdoor Play

Written and Illustrated by

Claudia Marie Lenart

To: Anahita ♡ Love Nature Claudia Marie Lenart

Loving Healing Press

Ann Arbor

Seasons of Joy: Every Day is for Outdoor Play
Written and Illustrated by Claudia Marie Lenart
Copyright © 2017 by Claudia Marie Lenart. All Rights Reserved.

To see her work, visit www.ClaudiaMarieFelt.com

ISBN 978-1-61599-317-8   paperback
ISBN 978-1-61599-318-5   hardcover
ISBN 978-1-61599-319-2   eBook

Published by
Loving Healing Press
5145 Pontiac Trail
Ann Arbor MI 48105

Tollfree 888-761-6268
Fax 734-663-6861

info@LHPress.com
www.LHPress.com

LOVING
HEALING
PRESS

Seasons of Joy is dedicated to
my mom, Clara Lenart, who,
by teaching me handwork arts
as a child, planted the seeds
for my future as a fiber artist.

Thanks to Ieva and Nicole
from DaVinci Waldorf School
in Wauconda, IL, for commis-
sioning my original Waldorf
seasons wool painting, which
inspired this book.

Wake up! It's Spring.

Trees are tipped in wisps of green.

Let's stretch our legs and run on soft, fresh
   grass.

Up and down the hills we hop and jump

Like newborn bunnies do.

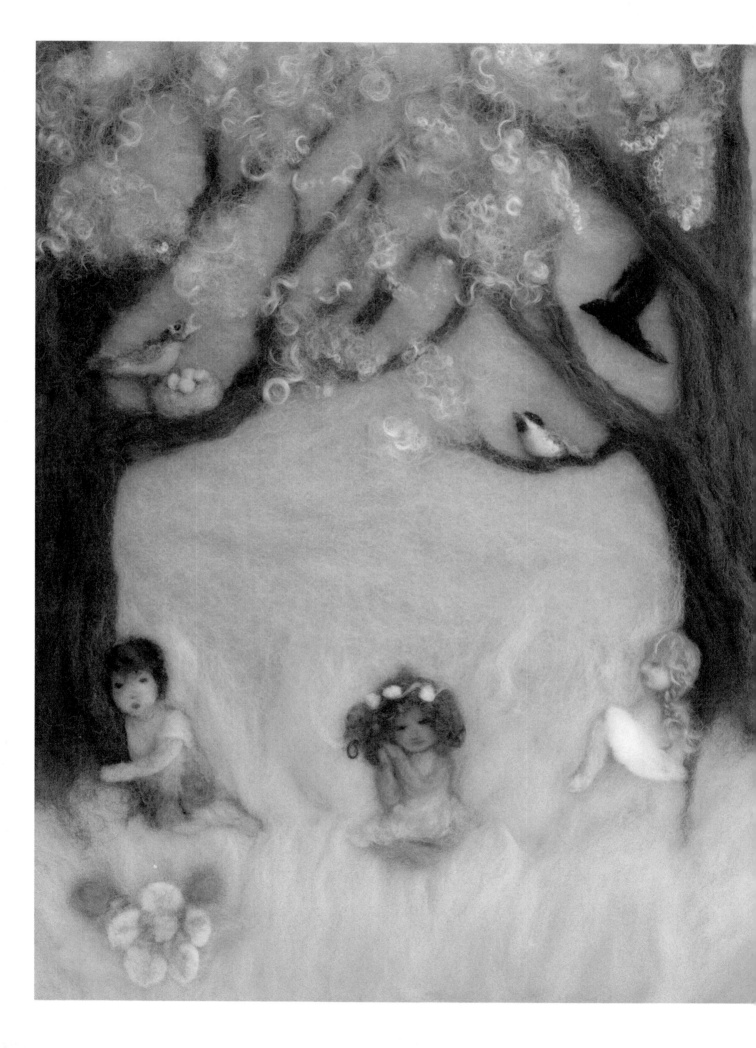

In Spring, the breezes are blossom sweet.

We close our eyes to hear a song in the sky.

Robin serenades her eggs with a lullaby.

Chickadees and blackbirds sing along,

Chicadee dee dee, Tu-a-wee, tu-a-wee.

In Spring, we picnic in velvet green meadows.

We pretend to be queens, kings, heroes.

The meadow is an emerald sea filled with pirates.

Our day is long; the world is fresh and beautiful.

We can dream anything.

It's Summer! There are endless days of light.

We float like happy otters swaying on the waves.

We water the garden and sprinkle each other.

We play hide-and-seek until the fireflies arrive.

And then we count the stars.

In Summer, we watch butterflies dance.

I can fly on my swing, high in the blue, blue sky.

You can fly too. I'll share my swing with you.

Let's climb the limbs of trees

To see the world as birds do.

In Summer we can play all day.

We create a tiny world with sticks and stones.

We make a fairy garden and a soft mossy bed

Where our fairy can rest her tiny head,

And dream, dream, dream.

It's Autumn! The leaves twirl to the ground.

We sway to the wind's song under crimson
showers.

We pile the leaves high in a great big mound.

We jump in. Leaves scatter. We pile them high
again.

Our fall circle game.

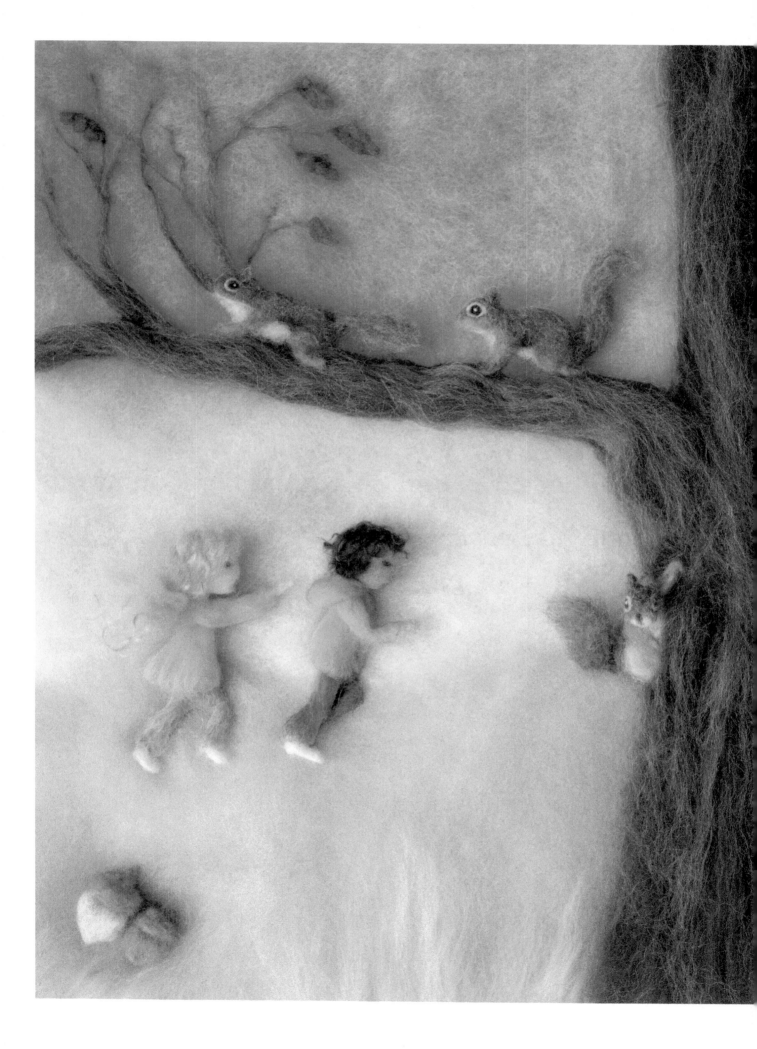

In Autumn, we are treasure hunters.

We discover a bounty of acorns, walnuts and

pine cones.

We are busy as squirrels scampering up trees.

They chase each other, a never-ending game

of tag.

Let's play that game, too.

In Autumn, we harvest our garden.

When the sky sends rain showers

We climb to the shelter of our treehouse.

We play until the sun paints the trees a
   copper hue.

Our day is shorter now.

It's Winter! The trees sparkle like fairy dust.

We throw our hands up to the sky.

We fall on our backs into pure, soft snow.

We flutter our wings.

We are angels.

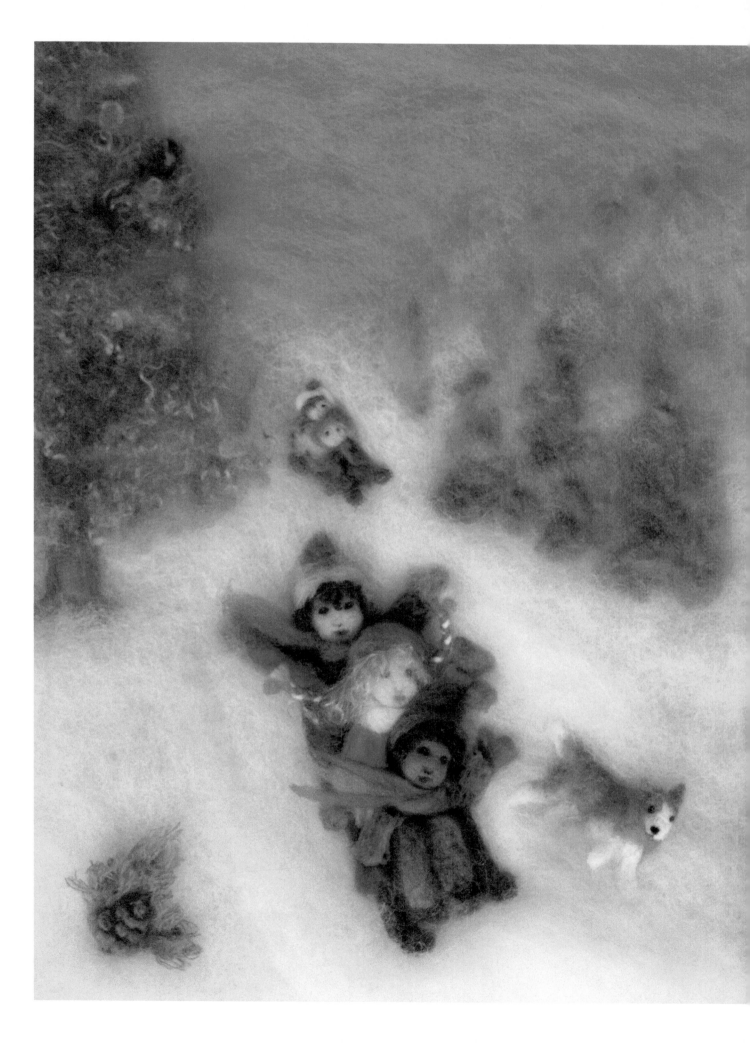

In Winter, the snow covers our world

With a fluffy white blanket.

We ride the hills on sleds

So fast, so fast, snow cascades our faces and

we laugh.

Our winter world so full of joy.

In Winter, we build a snow castle for little snowmen.

Soon we seek shelter, too, for the light is not long.

We are sleepy and nap like bears, dreaming of spring

And all the wonders of playing outside

All the joy the seasons bring.

About the Author

Claudia Marie Lenart is a fiber artist from northern Illinois. She experimented in the arts and handwork since childhood and while working as a journalist. While her son was in Waldorf school, she discovered needle felting and found her true passion.

Her soft sculpture characters are created by repeatedly poking wool and other natural fibers, like alpaca, with a barbed needle. Claudia pioneered a distinct style of illustrating books using wool as the medium. She illustrated three books for the late children's author Jewel Kats.

Claudia is a nature enthusiast and spent three summers working in national parks out west as a young adult. Daily walks in the woods with her dog inspire her wool paintings and wildlife sculptures.

To see her work, visit
www.claudiamariefelt.com

More magical needle felted illustrations by Claudia Marie Lenart

Jenny, a young girl undergoing treatment for cancer, discovers that her best friend, Dolly, also has cancer. Dolly is the family's dog, who has always been at Jenny's side through trying times, and Jenny vows to support Dolly as well.

This bittersweet tale is a story of mutual devotion and loyalty. While the prognosis is not good for dogs with cancer, Dolly's love provides enduring hope and support for Jenny on her healing journey.

Jenny & Her Dog Both Fight Cancer: A Tale of Chemotherapy and Caring
ISBN 978-1-61599-279-9

The King and Queen of Puppy Kingdom are joyfully awaiting the arrival of their Prince. But the couple and their kingdom are thrown into upheaval when it is learned that Prince Puppy will arrive early, before his important crown is completed. How can they call him Prince without a crown?

Discover how the King solves this problem in *Prince Preemie: A Tale of a Tiny Puppy Who Arrives Early*. Children will be swept away into this dreamy, fairy tale land of adorable dogs created from wool.

Prince Preemie: A Tale of a Tiny Puppy Who Arrives Early.
ISBN 978-1-61599-306-2

Join Hansel & Gretel in a world where courage and kindness overcome adversity

Hansel & Gretel: A Fairy Tale with a Down Syndrome Twist is an enchanting tale about how kindness overcomes callousness and leads to a wondrous reward.

This adaptation of the classic Grimms' tale includes the wicked witch and the poor siblings in search of food, but in this case, five-year-old Hansel is a mischievous, yet courageous, boy with Down syndrome.

Hansel and Gretel: A Fairy Tale with a Down Syndrome Twist
ISBN 978-1-61599-250-8

CPSIA information can be obtained
at www.ICGtesting.com
Printed in the USA
LVOW05*1359070417

529977LV00009B/35/P